Hello UP There!

Judi Buenaflor

AuthorHouse™
1663 Liberty Drive
Bloomington, IN 47403
www.authorhouse.com
Phone: 1 (800) 839-8640

Published by AuthorHouse 09/14/2018

ISBN: 978-1-5462-6000-4 (sc)
ISBN: 978-1-5462-5999-2 (e)

Library of Congress Control Number: 2018910987

authorHOUSE®

HELLO UP THERE!

A Story of Jimmy and the Giraffe

by Judi Buenaflor

Illustrations by Carol Kelley

"We're going to the zoo tomorrow. Did you remember, Jimmy?" "How could I forget, Mommy? I have been thinking about the giraffes all week." "Giraffes?" said Mom. "Why just giraffes? The zoo has so many wonderful animals: monkeys, fancy birds, lions, elephants, and bears. Don't you want to see all of the animals?"

"Sure, Mommy, but I really can't wait to see the giraffes. They are so tall. They can see everything. I want to be as tall as a giraffe."

Mom looked at Jimmy with sad eyes, then kissed him on the cheek. She left the den and went back into the kitchen to start dinner. She couldn't help but remember the accident that put Jimmy in a wheelchair. She and Jimmy talked often about it and are thankful that he is alive. She knows that Jimmy is still sad, though.

The sunlight streamed into Jimmy's bedroom. Mom came in.

"It's Saturday, Jimmy. You know what we are doing today?!"

Jimmy looked at his Mom and gave her a big smile. At last, he was going to get to see the giraffes.

It was a beautiful warm day. The sign for the zoo suddenly appeared when the car turned the corner of Oak and Elm Streets. Jimmy could not help but smile. He was finally going to see the giraffes up close.

Jimmy's Mom parked the car, got his wheelchair out of the trunk, and Jimmy, with the help of his Mom, bounced into the chair. He couldn't wait to get going.

After they went through the Entry Gate, Jimmy insisted that they visit the giraffes first.

When they got there, Jimmy catches sight of a giraffe right near the fence. He's eyes follow up the majestic animal's neck until they fall on its face. Without thinking, Jimmy blurts out, "Hello up there!"

Jimmy's Mom laughs, "Why did you say that?"

"He's looking at me, Mom. He looks like he wants to say 'Hello,' too."

Still laughing, Jimmy's Mom tells him that she wants to get a map of the zoo. The Information Booth is just down the path, she notes. As she starts to turn Jimmy's wheelchair around, he pleads,

"Mom, please let me stay here by the Giraffes while you get the map. You can see me from the Booth and I can see you."

Realizing that he was right, Jimmy's Mom agreed and locked the wheels of his wheelchair so it would not roll away.

"I'll be back in just a minute," she said.

"Okay."

As Jimmy's Mom walks away, he turns back to the Giraffe. Suddenly he hears

"Well, hello down here."

Jimmy's eyes get big with surprise and his mouth drops open.

"Did you just say Hello to me?" asks Jimmy.

"Why, of course," said the Giraffe. "You said 'Hello' to me and I did not want to be rude."

Jimmy's mouth now formed a big smile.

"It's so good to see you smile," said the Giraffe. "I know you haven't smiled very much since you've been in a wheelchair."

"How did you know that?" asked Jimmy.

"I know lots of things about you, Jimmy, and I'm glad you came to see me today so we could talk."

Just then, Jimmy's Mom returned with the map of the zoo.

"Let's go to the Monkey House," she said.

"No, please Mom," said Jimmy, "I want to stay here with the giraffes for a while longer."

"But there are so many different animals to see here at the zoo," said his Mom. "Don't you want to see them all?"

"Not now," Jimmy said. "I want to stay here."

Jimmy's Mom looked puzzled, but she agreed to let him stay with the Giraffes for a while longer. She found a bench close by and sat there to look over the map.

"I know that you have been very sad since your accident," said the Giraffe, "and that you will always be in a wheelchair from now on, so it's good to see you smile at me."

"Can you tell me what it is like to be as tall as you and see everything?" asked Jimmy. "I can't see much anymore since I must sit all of the time. I can't even climb high if I want to see something special."

"Yes, it's true, Jimmy, I can see far and over lots of things, but you can, too," replied the Giraffe.

"How?" asked Jimmy.

Now, the Giraffe smiles and says, "Jimmy, you can soar high with your imagination."

"My imagination?" replies Jimmy, "I don't understand."

"What do you think I see, Jimmy?" asks the Giraffe.

Jimmy looks around at the zoo.

"The sign for the Monkey House, the elephants, the zebras, and the parking lot.

"Jimmy," say the Giraffe, "close your eyes and imagine that you are sitting in that tree on the highest branch. What do you see?"

Jimmy does as the Giraffe asks and closes his eyes.

"I can see the sign for the Monkey House. I can see the elephants and the zebras. I can see the parking lot where our car is," Jimmy shouts with great excitement.

"If I were at your house, what would I see?" asks the Giraffe.

"My school and the playground and Noah's house," replies Jimmy.

"Jimmy," says the Giraffe, "imagine that you are on the roof of your house. What do you see?"

"I can see my school and the playground and the house of my best friend, Noah."

"See," says the Giraffe, "your imagination lets you see the same things I see."

"You don't have to be up high to see everything. Let your imagination lift you up."

"Close your eyes again," says the Giraffe. "What can you see in the zoo from where you are?"

"I can hear the lions roaring and I can see them pacing. I can hear the birds and see them flying."

Jimmy's smile got even bigger now because he understood what the Giraffe was telling him.

The Giraffe nodded and winked at Jimmy.

"Come on, Jimmy." said his Mom rising from the bench. "We had better get moving if we want to see all of the animals. I promise that we will stop to see the Giraffes again before we leave."

Jimmy smiles at his Mom and says, "OK."

Releasing the brake on his wheelchair, Jimmy rolled over to his Mom and slowly they made their way through the zoo. Jimmy never stopped smiling for the whole day because he could see EVERYTHING!

CPSIA information can be obtained
at www.ICGtesting.com
Printed in the USA
BVHW02s2055250918
528487BV00007B/16/P

9 781546 260004